Moment of truth

One day I went to a friend's birthday party and it was at an ice rink, and in rented figure skates two sizes too big I found out at last what I might do something special at. My dad was not there, but plenty of people told him when he came to pick me up, in fact they *ran* to tell him, even congratulate him, and he had no idea at first. But it was enough people, and enough of them were jock dads, that he started to get the idea, and then get interested.

We didn't talk about it on the way home until he brought it up, though you can bet I was excited beyond belief and wanted to do nothing but tell him. "They say you skate pretty," he finally said.

BILLY

Other Novels by Bruce Brooks

Asylum for Nightface

What Hearts

Everywhere

No Kidding

Midnight Hour Encores

The Moves Make the Man

THE WOLFBAY WINGS

Woodsie

Zip

Cody

Boot

Prince

Shark

BILLY

BRUCE BROOKS

A LAURA GERINGER BOOK

HarperTrophy®
A Division of HarperCollinsPublishers

Harper Trophy® is a registered trademark of
HarperCollins Publishers Inc.

Billy

Library of Congress Cataloging-in-Publication Data
Brooks, Bruce.
    Billy / by Bruce Brooks.
        p.   cm. — (The Wolfbay Wings ; #7)
    "A Laura Geringer book."
    Summary: With the support of his teammates behind him,
Billy tries to find the courage to stand up to his overbearing,
sports-obsessed father and reach his full potential as a hockey
player.
    ISBN 0-06-440707-1 (pbk.) — ISBN 0-06-027899-4 (lib. bdg.)
    [1. Hockey—Fiction.   2. Fathers and sons—Fiction.   3. Self-
confidence—Fiction.]   I. Title.   II. Series: Brooks, Bruce.
Wolfbay Wings ; #7.
PZ7.B7913Bi   98-14228
[Fic]—dc21   CIP
                                                                AC

Typography by Steve Scott
1   2   3   4   5   6   7   8   9   10
❖
First Edition

Visit us on the World Wide Web!
http://www.harperchildrens.com

BILLY

ee, I wasn't supposed to play hockey at all, I was supposed to do football, of course, because that's the one he says, like, "rips you to pieces until you're nothing but a bunch of crunched-up nuts and bolts in a pitiful pile of pain, and then football puts you back together again, piece by piece, until you're the man you're supposed to be, straight and tight and shining." My dad played football, see.

But the only thing was, I couldn't throw a spiral. This was crucial because I was not nearly big enough to go for line even with these injections my dad said he knew how to get for me if it would do any good, and he said I was not quick enough for cornerback or safety or fast enough for wideout, and runners got injured too much and as for linebacker—well, he would just chuckle and shake his head and say, "Linebackers are *born* linebackers, son, and you would have shown us by now if you were linebacker material, believe me." I was always a little disappointed when he said this because *he* looked disappointed, and I always wished I knew something to do that showed I *had* been born a linebacker, like throw my cereal bowl through the window or holler "YAAAHHHH! KILLLLLL!" or something linebackers hollered. (But I never hollered "YAAHHH! KILLL!" or anything, because if you hollered the wrong thing it would show you were *not* one of them even *more*, right?)

So, anyway, then it was supposed to be quarter-back for me—that was all that was left. "It's all right," my dad reassured me with a heavy pat on the back. "Quarterbacks can be useful." So on my fifth birthday we started, with a real football, small but leather and fully inflated too, so it felt like it was made of frozen wood when I caught it against my ribs or held it in my hands.

It felt okay in my hands, really, just holding it. But quarterbacks don't hold. They throw—the slant, the down-and-in, the square-out, the fly. And when they throw, the ball has *zip*, see, or some-times, on the long ones, it has *loft*. Nice words. But that's all they were, to me. Because when I threw the football, my elbow kept getting ahead, or be-hind, or my grip had too much squeeze or too little spread, or my fingertips failed to hold control, or *something*—and my passes, the ones that were supposed to zip or the ones that were supposed to loft, didn't matter which, they all spun sideways like the blades of a helicopter.

For the first of what became ten thousand times, my dad started saying, like he was confused at some trick I must be doing on purpose, "The foot-ball, son, was *designed* to spiral; it is very difficult to *keep* it from spiraling, if you *wanted* to, if you *tried* not to spiral it." But I would keep chucking these half-speed whirlybirds as my dad streaked down the sideline for the fly pattern and had to pull up short and watch the bounces, or cut sharply for the down-and-in and watched behind him as the ball went down and out, slowly.

I tried to get to *know* the football with my fin-gers: I held one all day long and when I slept too. Gripped right—my dad checked, all the time; I even ate left-handed so I could hold it, right there next to my salad plate. The grip—correct. The pres-ence—constant. But then the throws—whirlybird.

Eight months and he gave up on me.

Even so, even though he said he gave up, he signed me up for a league when I was six, saying maybe a coach would straighten me out, after all *he* (my dad) was just an ol' linebacker, what did *he* know about the subtle mechanics of release, as he called them. But after the first practice, during which I threw the ball exactly twice but did a bunch of other things besides, the coach found my spot and put me there, and as far as I was concerned in our first scrimmage that day he had picked pretty right. This coach—he was bald and skinny and wore blue mirror sunglasses—looked at me and saw I was not really big, saw I was slow, saw I could not throw or catch or tackle, saw that all I could do is get in somebody's way for a second or two.

But my dad was furious and pulled me off the team for good as soon as practice ended, and was very sarcastic all the way home.

"Tight end!" he snorted. "Tight end, everybody knows what you got is just a wideout can't do his job. A klutz. Some teams"—he looked at me—"some teams don't even bother to *have* them."

My dad will tell you flat out he did not have

enough to stick in the big time. He does not make it sound like more than it was. I mean, sure, he lets people know he played in the NFL, who wouldn't? But he always laughs and says he was just a linebacker a step too slow and made the rounds of the special teams squads for four years and that was it. Still. I mean—pretty good, right? He's on one of the promo ads, probably always will be, on three of the all-time hits videos too, for the same hit. Rookie kid just refused to call for a fair catch on a punt and he caught it, but my dad was already in the air aimed at his chin and my dad went *through* him. Kid's helmet came off, flying off, ball went straight up, and the kid turned a pure flip. You can see it twenty times a year.

You never see my dad after the hit, though. Know why? He kept running to go get the helmet, the kid's helmet he knocked off. Kept it too. No one ever asked for it back. The kid quit—*he* didn't want it. It's in the basement right now. My dad knew he'd done something pretty special.

I wanted to do something special too. But for me. Something that would be *mine*.

Then one day I went to a friend's birthday party

and it was at an ice rink, and in rented figure skates two sizes too big I found out at last what I might do something special at. My dad was not there, but plenty of people told him when he came to pick me up, in fact they *ran* to tell him, even congratulate him, and he had no idea at first. But it was enough people, and enough of them were jock dads, that he started to get the idea, and then get interested.

We didn't talk about it on the way home until he brought it up, though you can bet I was excited beyond belief and wanted to do nothing but tell him. "They say you skate pretty," he finally said.

Trying not to blurt it all out I said, "I just took that first step on the ice and it was, like, this is it, this is where I am supposed to, like, *be*." It was frankly hard not to scream in joy at the incredible show I had put on, of totally unprepared grace and speed and balance and imagination. I *spiraled*. By the end of the first hour, just before the pizza and cake, I even figured out how to skate backwards by myself, and by the end of the party I was crossing over, front and back. I never had a single thought out there, either. I just moved. There was no doubt—

I was what they called a natural.

And everybody made sure my dad knew it. I didn't have to brag. He thought a long time. "Well," he finally said, pulling his lip and thinking, "I guess there's hockey."

"Ice hockey?"

"They hit in hockey," he said, as if to himself. "Hit pretty good, pretty tough guys," he said starting to warm himself up to the idea. "Sure they do. Big smackeroos, and against those boards and glass and stuff too. Yeah, sure. I knew a guy on the Rams, grew up in Minnesota, and come to think of it he hit like a van hauling sand." He looked over at me. "Yeah," he said. "Maybe so. Maybe we'll do ice hockey and see if it's worth it."

We got in a league. I played. It was easy. The stick and puck felt as natural as the skates. My first two years I skated better than anybody on the ice on any team and scored a million goals, and though they didn't allow checking officially I hit some people hard, hard enough to make my dad happy, worth the penalties. He told me to slash them a little too with the blade of my stick, to see what I could get away with, "test the limits," he called it, "lay the lumber on the chap until it hurts him but you still get to stay on." I slashed a lot, got pretty good as soon as the ref turned his head. Nobody much liked me, including my coach from last year, but who cares, we sucked last year.

"There's many a fine team filled with players and coaches who hate only one thing worse than each other," my dad always said. "Losing."

My dad didn't really agree much with Coach Cooper's way of doing things and the way things kept going at the beginning, which was that we got killed every game, you couldn't really blame him for thinking maybe some other plan might work better. The big thing that got my dad furious was the way Coach Coop would set his lines and their rotation at the beginning of the game and stick with it all the way through. He had a special penalty-killing unit but that was the only time he messed with his regular rotation. I mean, like, if the other team's good line skated a long shift and was beat and skated off, and it happened to be the turn for our Spaz Line to go on, instead of sending our best line out to take advantage of the other guys' fatigue Coach Coop would go with the spazzes every time, end of the game, didn't matter. He explained at the start of the year that he was going to do that and that there would be many times it seemed stupid, but as he put it, we were a team on which every player had to be assured of his time or else a lot would get very little and they deserved to play too. It sounded great at the time but I have to go with my dad, it was plain stupid, especially when every other team jiggled and juggled and mixed and matched, always looking for an advantage.

Well, my dad decided to do a little silent or maybe just subtle subbing on his own. He offered to sit on the bench and run one of the gates for line changes, and sometimes when a good player was coming off but my dad saw he was still fresh and his replacement was worthless my dad would wink at the kid and whisper for him to stay out a little longer. Or maybe if a shift of bad players was skating by he would real sharp whisper the name of the guy who was skating by the bench and send me in and I would catch up and get in a little extra time. In fact he did this pretty often, yanking a forward near the bench and throwing me in there.

"You earn it," he said. "By being better than

whatever useless bag of pads Cooper has out there. By being, God forbid, *dangerous* a little. Something called a *threat*."

It got to be pretty open. My dad would yank guys and they might not bitch about it because they knew I was in fact better, but the leaders of the team, the best players, the guys my father didn't like at all because he said they only knew how to lead downhill, they started howling. Being on the ice I missed most of what they said but sometimes they waited until I got back to the bench and then they said stuff. At first it was kind of polite for them, like "Geez, didn't know we had a new coach," or something. But my dad seemed to be itching for more of a fight, and when they said stuff like that he would say "Any coaching would help, but not enough with a team full of chickenhearts," or "That wasn't coaching, that was common sense, just like what you did on your last shift wasn't hockey, it was common laziness." I can see how the guys got mad pretty fast when this is what he said to them, and they started speaking their minds in ways that made it clear my dad had the fight he wanted. They were not mean to me personally. They never treated me any different. I was a *Wing*, man. But they would say, "Hey, Billy, pardon me for mentioning it, but do you know what the difference is between your father and a sack of pig poop?" I either wouldn't answer or I would shake my head once and they would say, "Yeah, neither do I." Stuff like that.

Then suddenly one day my dad did not take the sticks under his arm like he always did and walk across the ice to the bench. He just sat in the stand, arms spread way out, chewing gum like he didn't care. I was already skating warm-ups, and I tapped the glass where he was a couple times and made a sign like "What's up?" but he ignored me. The game started. Changes were messed up because we only had somebody on one door, but still Coach Cooper didn't get my dad back out.

On the way home I asked what happened. He was still smacking his gum and grinned but it was fake. "I got fired," he said.

"But you didn't have a job."

"Exactly." He winked at me. "You catch on fast."

"So—"

"So you skate your shifts and nothing else and

Prince and Cody don't skate any more than Ernie and Shark and everybody's happy." He smacked his gum. I knew what I was supposed to say.

"And we get killed."

"And you get killed."

"'We're like happy and we're losing 17–1 all the time, but we're happy?'"

"You're happy and you're losing 17–1. All the time. Yes. You *love* to lose 17–1 in fact, because it proves you're a *gentleman*." This last word came out nasty enough that I didn't need to ask if it had come up between him and Coach Cooper.

But you couldn't keep my dad down. One day the ref—the *ref*, not the coach—leaned over the boards before the game and asked if anyone would run our penalty box. Before the sentence was over my dad was down there, but looking very casual about it. Well, the penalty box is not separated from the ice by glass so at least he was back giving tips to players as they skated close and when anyone got a penalty he pretty much talked to the guy the whole time. He was trying to help, see.

The players didn't see it. They had a lot of funny things to say when they got back to the bench from the box, slightly changing something my dad had said and making it stupid or extreme or more often dirty. Once, trying not to get mad because after all they never got mad at me for how he was, I asked Dooby, "So what's so bad if he sees something and tells you?"

"Billy, has he ever told you anything without making you feel like a moron first?"

"Well, sure—"

"Then we're just unlucky we're not his sons too," Dooby said.

Barry was sitting beside me and he leaned over and said, "Your dad, like, believes you have to kind of clear a player's head before he'll listen to the tip you want to give him."

"So?"

"So he believes you clear a guy's head fastest by telling him he's a fool or a piece of dead meat or something encouraging like that. Like, you get him ready for your message by humiliating him, *zap!*" said Prince.

"Does it work?" I asked. Everybody looked at me and I could see them thinking.

"No," said Dooby.

"Negatory," said Prince.

"Not for me," Cody said.

"Me neither," said Woodsie.

"Why not?" I asked.

There was a pause, and Dooby kind of looked very quickly at everyone like getting their okay to speak frankly, and he said, "You can only be humiliated by someone whose opinion you respect. I mean, if Jacques-Yves Cousteau told me my backhand sucked worse than a girl throwing a baseball, I wouldn't listen to him *either*, see? It's, like, not his *field*."

"Hey, if I ever want to learn how to cream guys on punt returns, though—" said Cody.

The year before last season with the Wings I played Mites. It was travel and everything, but I knew I was the only Squirt not to have also been a Squirt the year before. The reason I mention it is, in Mites, dads always come in and help their kids get all the pads and stuff on right, and they tighten their skates. I don't know why, there's something about it, but I only ever met one Mite who could tighten his own skates tight enough. If one dad was especially good at it he'd get asked to tighten three or four pair. My dad did only mine. He was great at it, but he didn't want to let anybody else know, I guess.

Anyway when I made Squirts my dad just kind of naturally kept coming in the locker room and helping me get my stuff on, like holding one shin guard and handing it to me as soon as I had taped the first one on, or handing me my second elbow pad. The two back snaps of my helmet's chinstrap were really hard to reach and put any pressure on, so he snapped those. And he tightened my skates.

It took me a while but all of a sudden one day I noticed no other dads ever came into the locker room to help their kids. Most of them never showed their faces—the kids walked in with their own bags and got down to it and hit the ice all tightened and snapped and ready.

Except me.

My dad never seemed to notice, but I did. The talk was a little stiffer, a little more careful and less relaxed, like there was an intruder in the conversation or something. Considering the way my dad got along with some of the guys, I guess it's no surprise he made them uncomfortable by just being there.

But he didn't notice, just handed me my pads and when I was ready tightened my skates.

One day on the way home I asked him if he felt anything funny when he was in the room.

"Sure I do. I feel like I'm in the dressing room for a ballet recital, not a hockey game."

"No," I said, "I meant—"

"I know what you meant, of course," he snapped. "And of course I feel the discomfort the nice boys suffer from the presence of the big bad man breaking up their petty little clubby group-thing."

"We call it a 'team,'" I said, surprising myself.

He snorted as he laughed. "Call it that if you want. You might as well call it the state legislature." He laughed to himself. "The Joint Chiefs of Staff."

"I feel weird being the only one who gets helped."

"Can you tighten your skates?"

"I don't know," I said. "I haven't tried."

"Do you like seeing your old man a few extra minutes before you enter the wars?"

"Of course."

"Well, then," he said. "I'd say it's nobody's business but ours."

But that night in my room, I tried tying my own skates. I got them tight enough, I thought. And I thought about those "extra minutes" and how they mostly consisted of my dad looking very bored holding out a piece of equipment to me without a word. In fact, he almost always left after snapping my helmet without saying a thing, like "Go at 'em hard, Ace!" or anything like that. The point is, it wasn't exactly a big quality thing for us.

The next day the room seemed especially quiet, the other players especially awkward. I felt bad enough that I promised myself I would talk to my dad again after practice and ask him to stop coming in.

But I didn't have to. I had put on everything but helmet, gloves, and skates, when Zip, walking like a fat boy in his goalie pads, strolled over, reached into my bag just ahead of my dad's hand, and pulled out my left skate. He looked me in the eye and held it out to me.

"Here you go, man. You're a Squirt, and Squirts tighten their own skates. And if you need your helmet snapped, I'll do it."

"What if he doesn't want you to?" said my dad,

smiling. Zip was still looking at me, holding out the skate.

He shrugged. "Cody'll do it. Or Prince. Or Barry. Or Shinny. Somebody who is also a hockey player, like he is, will do it. In the meantime, it's a disgrace about the skates."

I took the skate from him. "Sorry," I said. "I can get them tight enough just fine."

"No problem," said Zip, turning and walking off. "We just thought we'd give you a while to get used to it and now that little while is up."

"You said a 'hockey player' is going to help him if he needs it," my dad started.

"Yes," sighed Zip, "and you don't see any hockey players in the room. Hahaha. Why don't you go practice being a hockey father? And if you want to tighten anything, try your necktie."

My dad stood up and stuck his finger in Zip's face. Zip backhanded it away. My father stuck it back, and Zip backhanded it again, no harder, just hard enough.

"What you need," said my dad, "is somebody who isn't afraid to whup your tail until you learn how to be a boy."

"I thought the whole idea was to grow up and become a man," said Zip, looking my dad in the eye. "Or isn't that right?"

"You've got a long way to go," said my dad, pivoting on his heel and walking straight out the door.

"So does Billy, but it just got a lot shorter, thanks," Zip hollered after him.

ne day we gave Woodsie a ride home. It was about in the middle of the year which matters because Woodsie had not played hockey before this year and sort of sucked at first or at least looked like he sucked and for a defenseman looking like you suck looks very bad but he was watching and thinking and picking stuff up all the time and by a third of the way through he was suddenly always in the right spot, always, and he was becoming the kind of passer who sees three steps ahead of everybody except the guy he passes to. He is a very nice guy, pretty quiet, only says something when it counts. My father started the year hating him—he talked Woodsie up as his favorite example of how Coach Coop was committed to losers. But after a while I noticed my dad stopped saying much about Woodsie.

Woodsie is not the kind of kid who would ever show he did not like someone just fine: He was very polite and good at listening to grown-ups, so it wasn't like taking Zip for a ride or something. I thought it was a pretty safe bet that things would go smooth.

As soon as we were rolling, with Woodsie in the back, my dad looked at him in the mirror and said, "Be a center next year."

I didn't twist around so I don't know what Woodsie did, but I heard some typical kind of apologetic mumbles and I gathered he was saying he thought he'd stick with D.

My father was still talking at him through the mirror, shaking his head. "No money in D, my friend." Woodsie said something and my father went on. "You can say that now but what about ten years from now? When the centers like Billy here are getting the big ones and you're backskating, backskating, backskating, making a fifth of what they do? I know it seems like a long time, but—"

"Excuse me," said Woodsie, in a loud voice for him plus he interrupted, which he never does. "I really am not prepared to consider hockey as—"

"Well, you should," my dad said, interrupting *him*. "You should. I misjudged you, and I admit it here and now—I thought you had nothing more than what showed, and showed early. But let me tell you something, my friend." Here my dad waited to make sure he had Woodsie's eyes in the mirror, I guess. "Let me be the first to tell you: You have *got* it. You have all the things they can't teach, so all you have to do is learn what they *can* teach and you are going to be—" My dad shook his head, like he couldn't express how big. He sighed, and looked out the windshield for a while. "Rink sense. It's unreal. You—at any moment you know just where you are in relation to the blue lines and red line and boards *and* you know the same thing about all the other players out there too. Hands. Jeez, the touch you put on the smallest pass—" He shook his head again.

"Excuse me, but it's to the left here," said Woodsie. "Then right in a block."

"Get that boob to move you for the rest of the year," my dad said, glancing in the mirror.

"This is it right here," said Woodsie, opening the door almost before the car stopped. "See you, Billy. Mr. Fowler, thanks a lot for the—"

"You could pick up thirty, forty assists, score

twenty-five, thirty-five goals."

Woodsie had almost shut the door, but he stopped and left it open six inches.

"Guess what?" he said.

"Me? Me guess?" said my dad.

"Yes," said Woodsie.

My dad laughed kind of nervously. "I don't know, what?"

"I like to watch hockey," said Woodsie. "That's what."

"But what in the—"

"And when I am playing defense—which, by the way, has satisfactions every bit as profound as the assist or the goal—when I am playing defense, where am I?"

"Where? Well, you're—"

"It's all in front of me," Woodsie said. "I get to watch it all unfold. Maybe I get to *make* it unfold, but still—nothing's going on behind my back. There's no part of the ice I'm allowed to ignore. Anyway—you see?" He smiled. "I get the double thrill. I get to play the game, and I get to watch the game. Two for one. Thanks. 'Bye now."

He closed the door and got his bag and sticks

out of the trunk and walked away. My father muttered.

"So he likes D," I said. "Big deal."

"I just wish to God you had half his rink sense and half his touch," said my dad, heaving a sigh and slamming the car into reverse. "Then you'd *really* make some jack."

"But you think I'm going to make *some*, anyway? I mean, you think I got what it takes—"

"What you got is, you skate pretty and you shoot nice and straight," said my dad. "Enjoy yourself and your hockey endeavors. Now I got to think for a while."

That was it. We rode home in silence.

By halfway through the season my dad was already talking about summer hockey camp for me. On the way home from practice he would go drill by drill and say why Coach Cooper had no idea how to build a player or a team, just wait, this summer he would find me some training, some workouts, someone who would see what he could make out of me, just wait, he had a few things to investigate. . . .

Turns out the camp he picked was the one run by a guy named Marco who coached against us but had a much better team. Marco used to play pro, not the way my dad played pro football, on taxi squads for a couple of years, but Marco was like *good* for ten years in the NHL, a tough winger with scars all over his face and totally false teeth and hands that looked horrible. "See those knuckles?" my dad asked me. "Those are the bad knuckles of a bad man who knew how to take care of himself.

Those knuckles have banged a few bones." He always got pretty enthusiastic talking about how tough Marco was.

Marco ran a camp for one week, all day every day, going hard the whole time. He ran it twice, in case you couldn't make the first one or something. But my dad had what he thought was the genius idea of signing me up for *both* weeks, repeating everything, because it would "keep your skates on the ice" and I don't know what all else. On the first day of the first week I was really glad (my dad was not) to see that a bunch of the guys from my team, the Wings, were coming to the camp too.

But I found out none of them was signed up for both weeks. In fact, they thought the idea was nuts.

"Marco and his boys *kill* you for the week," said Dooby. "They run your tail to the bone. By Friday you *hate* hockey."

My dad just smiled at that.

"And it cuts into goof time seriously," said Cody.

I could see my dad just nodding and thinking "So go ahead and have your goof time, and lose another thirty next year." Actually, it was twenty-nine.

And last my teammates kind of hinted there was a special way you needed to recuperate from the week, but before they told me about it they tried to convince me two weeks was just over the top. "Would you take Algebra I over again if you didn't have to?" Zip said. "Would you yank out a new filling and go right back just to sit in the dentist's chair and let him start drilling all over again?"

I kind of hinted this stuff to my dad, but he just grunted, and remarked about how players on teams that lost thirty games were players who hadn't gotten all their cavities filled yet. They did as little as they could get away with, then moaned about it and went somewhere and goofed off until all the good influence of the training had been thrown away and wasted.

But not me, he said. I was going to "take Marco's best shot" and come back for more. He was actually more pleased that there was no one else doing two weeks than if I had been going to have a teammate or two for company.

I wasn't more pleased, though.

On that first Monday morning of camp we hit the ice early, and I found out all the other Wing guys had done the camp the year before, some of them for a few years, so they knew what was coming. Plus there were guys from teams we played including some I had hated pretty bad, but now everyone was all friendly, Wings with Montrose players and Annapolis players and all. I'd be panting in line behind Dooby and another player, and we'd all start talking and the guy's turn would come to take off in the drill, and I'd say, "Seems like a good dude," and Dooby would say, "Funny you say that—he knocked you on your tail at least six times last year and the only time you tried to get him back you got nailed for a spearing major."

"You mean—"

"Yep. That was Number 9 from Reston."

"That jerk!"

"Only when he's wearing his uniform."

That's just how it was. We were all kind of one group, doing camp together. For me, maybe because it was looser, the togetherness thing was even better.

And camp was a nasty experience much of the time except for going through it with other guys. First hour, before you were even really awake, was "power skating" with this nice-looking plump lady wearing dippy white figure skates who had like spent her life inventing these bizarre skating motions you repeated until you discovered just how very hugely unbelievably *many* little muscles go into taking a stride on the ice, and how easy it is to hurt these little muscles, but never mind that. It felt farther from hockey than walking on your hands through hot sand would. You had no idea you were at *hockey* camp. No way. You were at *stretch those tendons on the outside of your ankles until they feel like a bandage* camp. Where Marco found her I do not know, but she was there waiting for us every morning, very nice, never angry, never yelling insults and slogans, that stuff they use in like football to make you "dig down deep" or whatever, nothing but, okay, you're at this end of the ice and you appear to be wearing ice skates so why don't you just go ahead and travel down to *that* end of the ice, but just to make it weird do it *this* way, swiveling *these* joints and using only *those* edges of your skates. Okay?

The second day I asked her. I said, "I'm pretty happy with the way I can skate when I play hockey, you know? I mean, I even think I skate pretty nice."

"Nice*ly*," she said. "Go on."

The other guys were just watching. I went on anyway. "Nice*ly*," I said. "So why do I have to do this? Isn't it even possible this might, like, mess up my, like, natural stride or something?"

She smiled. "Wearing thin blades on your feet and balancing on them precariously with an absurd perpendicularity and then trying to move with some command of various possible changes in direction and speed, can never be called 'natural,' son. Skating is as unnatural as it gets. Even *bowling* makes better sense. And when, on top of the ice skates, you throw in sticks and a puck, you *really* get strange. So, nothing I am having you do even comes close to how peculiar what you *want* to do is. And if you were doing something 'natural,' you would probably be lying down somewhere asleep."

And that was that. But for a couple of days a few guys started calling me "Mr. Natural," mainly Dooby. In the first scrimmage on Monday I had slashed him across the backs of his knees just to let him know I was there, but he stopped, turned and put his glove into my chest until I stopped too, then skated backwards counting to himself, and stopped. Then he quickly took the end of his stick in both hands and swatted my helmet like a baseball, probably almost as hard as he could. I went down screaming, but he leaned over me and said, "This is *camp*, Mr. Intensity. And if I want, I can slice your fingers off one by one with a skate blade and sell them back to you at immense profit. So get smart, okay? I don't want to see you slashing *anybody*. You can work hard and learn a lot of hockey but this is *vacation*, remember? I know your dad is an uptight bozo who probably asks every night how many people you hurt, but learn to lie, okay?"

So, okay, it's "camp" and we're all loose and cool? Okay, I can do that, I can have some fun. Rest of that shift in the scrimmage I pretty much steal the puck from one of my own linemates, and I just turn on the Pretty Skating, zipping in and out of danger but keeping just clear of it, and keeping the puck, hanging onto it, until I can score, and I score. Next shift I make sure I get the puck again, and this time there are a few people mad and so they try extra hard and that makes it even *more* fun to skate until they're foolish and then stick it. Two shifts, two goals, no congratulations. But moves—hey, plenty of moves, plenty of tension and thrills and almost-got-nailed and hey-I-sure-tricked-*you*-eh? all over the place. I avoid so many hip checks against the boards from this one defenseman who is determined to crunch me that he eventually beats himself off the ice, *bam bam bam*, where did that kid go to?

Over here, pal.

Ooops, now I'm here.

But not for long—I'm here now, and it's just me and the goalie and I wipe him out by shooting too early and too low and just too doggone accurate. Three.

Final score for the afternoon: six shifts, six goals, no friends, who cares? Fun. Lots of fun. Lots of making people look goofy. Tomorrow, I'm sure the teams will be rearranged or something, I won't be allowed to get away with this for long, but, hey, like Doober said, it's summertime, vacation, and skating away from everyone with the puck and then popping a goal is pretty good summertime fun. It sure isn't that too-intense stuff, is it?

The next morning Woodsie and Zip and Dooby and Cody walk over together as I'm getting my skates on.

"Had a meeting last night, Billy," says Zip.

I look up at him. "And?"

"And, you'll be glad to know, we decided to save you," says Woodsie.

"Maybe even to *like* you," Cody adds.

"Instead of what?" I say. "What are my other choices?"

Dooby shakes his head. "The choices are not yours."

"So, like, what, am I, suddenly a nice guy or something?"

"Yes," says Woodsie.

And they leave me with that.

That, and the one cheekbone . . .

From Dooby's hit, on one cheekbone I had red lines that turned purple in the pattern of the squares of my face guard, in addition to a headache for two days. Otherwise, fine. When my dad saw the lines he said, "You whack him back?"

"I whacked him *first*," I said, like I was kind of proud of it.

He shook his head like I had just thrown another unspiraling bomb at him on the fly pattern. "Never let anybody get last licks," he said. "First licks fade. Last licks last."

I did not slash Dooby back, however. And like I said, he was nicer to me after the slash-and-swat tradeoff, and everybody from the Wings, too. I didn't know why it made a difference that they got to see me get creamed, but my dad did—"Jealous, pal. Those boys been jealous of you since the first Squirt skate last fall. Anybody else move so pretty?"

"Cody," I said.

He was annoyed I answered him, it was one of those you aren't supposed to answer, but he blew Cody away anyhow with a backhanded wave. "Too low, too belly-to-the-ice, lots of speed but zero power for our friend the coach's son." He paused, then resumed his list of the things they were jealous of me for. "Anybody else get the puck on net with ninety-seven percent of his shots? I don't *think* so. Cripes, Prince must have an on-goal percentage below half; he missed some nets last year he should be able to hit from *twice* as far away as he was, with two more guys checking him. And how about that little extra edge of mean, huh? Anybody but that maniac goaltender show a *bit* of feeling out there last year, a bit of inclination to show an opponent that he was *hated* and when he played the Wings he was going to *pay*, with *pain*? If that Zip of a netminder could keep his stick to himself in situations where an obvious whack did him *no* good as far as the hockey went, except for him, you lead the team in PIM and for every minute you served you *ought* to have served fifteen, and that's what we want. You weren't nearly nasty and sneaky enough, but you'll learn, and they won't, not from nice Gentleman Coach Cooper-Dooper, and they saw it in you."

I was getting excited about all of this stuff, and I goofed by joining in. "And, like, one of the dads must have told me twenty times he like *loved* the fact I played with *style*. Talk about that. Talk about my style."

My dad winced. He shook his head very slightly. "I'm afraid you want to talk about style you better go down to the beauty parlor and get together over a cappuccino with a stylist, bub." He shook his head again. "I don't *see* style, see? I see skating, shots, goals, hits, whuppings—plain old stuff like that. Style? Style is for people who add up to nothing and have to give it a name."

I was a little disappointed, mainly because I had really *liked* thinking I played with style, but my dad sure didn't leave much room for keeping *that* pride in my mind any longer. But the rest of what he said made some sense—especially when you considered his final point, the one he always mentioned last to anyone he was telling about my hockey.

"And," he said, raising his eyebrows and one side of his mouth, "and don't kid yourself—they went over those birthdays on the roster, and they could add and subtract, and they couldn't get rid of the fact you were the youngest guy on the team by *eleven months*. Almost could have played Mites! And here you were, skating circles around kids, some of 'em two years older, been skating probably five *years* longer, but there you were, and you think they liked that?"

By now I knew enough not to really answer, so he shook his head himself. "No. No like. Billy too much too young, no like. No fit Coach's ideal of carrying a purse instead of a piece of lumber. No. And that's bound to carry over into camp, my boy. You still skate circles around them, you're still a year younger, they're still losers."

"Well," I said, "last season we *did*, like, get a lot better and stuff."

He shrugged. "They don't like you, Billy, that's all, and I'm just trying to show you it's nothing to be ashamed of. I'm not going to argue with you. You want to play hockey the way that team did last year, be my guest."

I had never thought the guys, like, really didn't *like* me the way he was saying, I mean, I knew I didn't fit in real easy all the time and some of them resented some of my penalties and a lot of them kind of joked about how excited I got when I started talking maybe a little too much or fast, but jeez. And now they had *really* taken me in.

That day at camp all of a sudden during lunch break I just asked Dooby. "Did you guys dislike me last season?"

He thought as he chewed his tuna sandwich. "I wouldn't say so, no," he said, "not really. You were probably in the middle third, low but in there, and that's acceptable. Your dad is crow food, but you're all right."

"Thanks."

"No problem." He took another bite.

I couldn't help asking one more thing. "Anything I could do to move up? Say to the higher level of the middle third?"

Dooby's mouth was full, so Zip answered, "Kill your dad." He smiled and nodded. "I have the feeling you'd blossom as an individual."

"Zip, come on," said Woodsie.

"All right, 'blossom' isn't a good hockey-guy word. You'd probably 'emerge.'"

A whistle blew and we had to tighten our skates and get back to the ice.

fter that first scrimmage, I changed to my clothes and was just about to go when I heard my name called from the open doorway of the office. I was pretty surprised and looked around, but nobody else was looking up, so I went over and stood there and peeked in. A couple of the assistant guys who ran drills were standing around and the lady was perched on one corner of this desk, but the main man in the room was Marco, who was sitting in the desk chair leaning back with his skates crossed in the middle of the desk and his hands behind his head and a cigar in his teeth. They all just looked at me. Marco was smiling.

"Um, yeah?" I said.

"You beat up Pelletier last year, didn't you?"

I swallowed. "So?" I said.

He laughed around his cigar. "Your coach tell you to?"

"No," I said. "I fight my own fights."

"You're not a very good liar," he said, "and I suspect you're even a nice enough kid. Tough," he added hastily, holding up a palm, "plenty tough, but a good guy. So I'm giving you a homework assignment."

"Homework?"

He nodded at a stack of about six videocassette cases on his desk and one of the assistants handed me one. "This is some fun stuff to watch. Half of it is taken during the pick-up game the All-Stars play before their real game, and half of it is from the Stanley Cup finals last year. I want you to look at it tonight, and tomorrow I want you to tell me what it is that hockey players do every single time they can, whether they are having pure fun or playing for the big bowl. Same thing, same fun. Never changes, no matter who the player is. Check it out, talk to me at lunch." He winked, and I knew it was time for me to go. As I left he hollered out another kid's name.

That night my dad and I watched the video. During the pick-up game the best players in the world did seem to be having fun like crazy, but I had to watch three times before I figured it out.

"They're *passing* as soon as they can," I said. "If somebody's two steps ahead they pass to him. And when they're set up they're showing off by being like creative with their passes, trying to get it to the guy with the very best shot. And laughing and stuff." In the Stanley Cup game film they were doing the same thing. I don't care who it was, superstar or not, he moved the puck forward as soon as he could by passing it ahead. If he was the superstar he usually got it *back*, down the line, but still.

My dad waved a hand at the set. "Phooey," he said. "You ask those guys what puts money in the bank and champagne in the Cup, and they'll tell you: Goals, goals, goals. Marco—he's playing with your head, holding you back a little for some reason, but don't worry, he'll cut you loose."

"But these guys on the tape—"

"You ever see them award a victory to the team with the most pretty passes in a game?"

The next day I returned the tape, but I didn't get a chance to tell Marco what I had observed. In the scrimmage I decided to try to show him, though, and I did like the guys on the tape, and every time I got the puck I was looking up to see if there was somebody better off to pass it to and I did. And like the stars on the tape, a lot of times a few passes later the puck came back to me and a few times I had pretty good shots. I scored *three* that day, but I only handled the puck about half as much.

"You get a pretty good grade on your homework," Marco said when he skated past me after scrimmage. "Remember it."

Passing the puck whenever possible had another effect. While we were getting dressed Dooby said, "Hey, I guess you're not just a total puck pig."

"So we've decided to take a chance," said Zip.

"A *risk*," said Dooby. "Because you may still be many other bad things."

"But—well, keep the slashing down and the passing up and you'll be a *real* Wing, and thus you will qualify for the official Wing Intensive Seasonal Preparation Week."

I looked at them all. Finally I asked, "What's that?"

"It's what we do during the second week of Marco's camp."

Zip said, "My family has this big house on Chincoteague, and every summer a select bunch of us go down and hone our hockey skills."

"Such as body surfing."

"And sitting in the shade of umbrellas and reading select parts of Henry Miller novels."

"And performing very girl-impressive diving catches of the Frisbee."

"And eating." They all groaned.

"Barbecue," said Dooby. "Zip's grandmother's barbecue."

"And his father's fried chicken."

"And crabs."

"Lots of crabs."

"Cooked by *anybody*."

"Jeez," I said. "It sounds like the *best*."

"Two newcomers have been selected for initiation this year, after careful review," said Zip. "Woodsie, and you."

"Needless to say, the most profound hockey-team bonding takes place as a running theme behind every activity."

"Except when Cody plays his guitar," said Barry.

"No," said Dooby, holding up a finger, "this

year *all* team members are invited to bring their own musical instruments. Remember our concert."

"Jeez," I said. I had never felt so accepted. Plus it sounded like more fun than I had had since third grade.

"Needless to say," said Zip, fixing me with a look, "it is only your company we invite. Not your father's."

"'You shoulda caught that wave thirty feet farther out, knucklehead!'" hollered Barry, in a surprisingly good imitation of my father. Even I laughed. Until I remembered my scheduled second week of Marco.

"I got a problem," I said.

Dooby gave me a wink. "But you'll get some help."

And for the moment I left it at that.

five

The middle part of every day at camp was the part I liked best, and most kids did too because you got to do so many things one at a time.

Plus you got to find out all these cool ways to cheat.

But first, the legitimate stuff. The guys who worked as Marco's assistants, mostly college hockey players I think, would set up five different stations around the ice, and each guy would be teaching one like isolated skill thing. We'd be divided into five groups and every twenty minutes or so Marco would blow his whistle and we'd go along to the next station. Marco kind of floated around between stations pointing things out, giving key tips and stuff. He never stayed in one place for long and I must say that for a camp with his name on it there really wasn't much feeling of being taught *by* Marco. But the college guys were good and the white-skates lady was radical, so it probably didn't matter much.

At one station we'd like work only on carrying the puck while turning in the direction of our backhand, pulling it backhand while we skated in circles around a line of four cones. At another station we'd do wrist shots, and the guy would break it all down into the parts of a shot, how you let yourself overskate the puck while you hold it on your forehand and at the same time slide it down to the heel of your stick blade, and then how you dipped a shoulder and rotated at the waist and balanced on this foot and ended up with your blade pointing at exactly the spot you wanted to puck to end up. Or we'd all drop the sticks and carry the puck through a curvy course between cones, only moving it with our skates. Probably more than anything else that drill helped me because it's the kind of thing you never practice or make yourself do when you are fooling around, but probably ten times a game you need to control the puck with your skate blade for any number of reasons. Sometimes a drill would use two or three of us—like for all of the different kinds of passing (one day we didn't even use a puck—all we passed back and forth in pairs was eggs! Only about five got broken.)

Most of these sessions were spent on offensive stuff. This was fine with me because I consider myself an offense player. But Zip kept moaning. "Hey," he'd shout at Marco skating by, "instead of teaching these bozos how to backhand eggs, how about you give them at least the idea of noticing a rebound that might be lying in the slot after the goalie has made a heroic save, and how it might be a good thing to kind of clear it away?" (Zip has a big thing about getting the puck cleared from in front of him. Looking at how many goals we allowed, and how good a goalie he actually is, I'd say he has a point.) Dooby and Barry also growled a lot about the emphasis on skills that had mostly to do with scoring. "Hip checks, even just those little 'Excuse me!' half-assed ones," Dooby said one day. "We could spend an entire *day* getting these whizzy high-scoring types to use the protoplasm below their numbers to maybe nudge a shooter off-balance or give a flying wing a little push toward the boards to keep him wide on a rush until the D got set in the middle, you know? Or maybe—hey, I don't ask for much—maybe just *one* session on how to sneak your hand through from behind a shooter who has beaten you to the puck-side in the slot, how to snake it through between his arm and body and just kind of grab ahold of his stick shaft so that when a centering pass came along—"

I think I kind of gasped. "But—but that's not *legal*, Dooby," I said. "That's, like, 'holding the stick,' you get a two-minute minor for that, right?"

I looked at the faces of the three or four guys around us. "Right, guys?" I asked again. None of them looked at me but finally somebody said, "Yeah, Billy, sure."

Then, after a pause that let the subject kind of die, one Easton defenseman said, in a voice he pretended was like half-apologetic, "One morning Marco *did* teach me this neat little trip you can pull when you're skating *ahead* of a guy and you think maybe he's going to outskate you to the puck."

"Cool!" said Dooby. "Now we're talking! Show us!"

I started to protest, "But trips are not—"

"Billy, let's practice some one-touch backhand passes," Woodsie interrupted, and then skated me about ten feet away and we passed back and forth while this Easton kid demonstrated to about six eager guys how Marco had showed him you could be skating ahead and looking ahead but just real quick let your stick drag behind your legstroke *between* your legs once instead of outside one leg like usual, and while it was back there you jammed it sideways and it hit the inside edge of the guy's skates behind you and down he went. I was really disgusted. Teaching people to trip!

But an hour later, racing this speedy little guy from Reston to the puck in the neutral zone, without really intending to, I tried it, just the way the Easton kid said Marco taught him. It worked perfect. The kid was upright one second, on his butt the next, and I had never even looked at him.

So what started to happen was, we would go and do our station drills and we *would* do them, really; but also, we started to ask Marco and then the college guys to show us stuff that was what you might call smart and practical but maybe kind of shady as far as pure ideal legal hockey went. Marco never acted shy about any of this insider stuff at all, the question of rules had no application, he was happy to show us what he always called The Great Game, but greatness as it was really played rather than the way it was written down in a book.

Far from pretending everything was pure and clean, he encouraged us to learn everything we could. Here's one great tip he gave us: "If a guy pulls a good one on you—an invisible trip, a hidden spear under the chest pads, a roll on your knees—don't get mad and waste time whining to the ref or slashing the guy's glove pads to show how mad you are. No. What you do is, you *copy* him. You *learn* the trick. Because if he can get away with it, chances are you can too." And then Marco would skate happily off to some other grouping.

People who know anything will always say, "Hockey is a defensive game." Obviously it's true— you see a lot more scoring in every other sport, even baseball. What people either don't know or don't tell you is that the defensive nature of hockey comes as much from frustrating highly skilled scorers with these tricks of unskilled crudity as it does from matching them skill for skill or devising some great strategy. I mean, sometimes it's like "If a guy is about to take a decent shot, hook his neck from behind and yank him down, hard." But if the refs don't call it and people keep on passing the tricks down generation to generation and they keep working, well, I guess the offensive players are doomed to whine without getting anybody to listen and pro games will keep winding up with scores like 3–2 which nobody complains much about.

I admit that I think about scoring more than anything and work most on the skills that lead to scoring chances, and I admit it doesn't occur to me all the time that I am supposedly covering another player whenever his team has the puck. I usually go my shift without even knowing which guy is mine. My dad says it's okay. "Anyone can grab a guy's jersey or stick a knee in his back or whack his stick so he doesn't get a shot off. But look around and tell me how many guys you see with the scoring touch? With the skills, the instincts, the stuff that makes the puck end up back there in the twine? Then tell me what statistic it is that makes one team get declared victorious at the end of a game. Most *goals*, isn't it? Makes it pretty clear, doesn't it? So you keep at it, you play your game—because as long as you can score you got a job on a good team."

But I got to say there is something so smart and skilled and tough and even flashy about the way a very good "defensive defenseman" plays the game, that by paying attention to a few at that camp I started to respect them as much as the highest scoring kids, easy. Three of them were my teammates: Barry, Dooby, and Woodsie *played*. They weren't just big trunks whose job it was to get in your way, like I used to think. For example, I bet Barry had stick skills as good as anyone's in camp. But he used them to poke-check, or to snatch the puck out of the corner, or to tip a dangerous shot out of the air so it angled off-goal. Dooby was one of the best guys there—make that *the* best—at using his backside and shoulders to keep players out of the positions they wanted to be in, whether he was carrying the puck and they were trying to reach it, or they were setting up to take a pass and he made them take it off-balance or further out than they wanted or get the puck and their own stick blades tangled in their skates because he gave them the perfect bump at the right time. Woodsie had two things: the best hands in camp—better than the guys who flipped in all the fancy shots—and he was the most creative passer. He made plays happen that would not have occurred to anybody if he hadn't made a certain pass that might even look pointless or dumb until you realized the kid who had to change direction and speed up to skate onto it was actually *now* in position for a strong forehand shot from the unprotected side of the defense.

The scrimmages definitely were competitive as they could be, but for sure they did not have any of the intensity of a season game or that sense of being on a team mission that you get game after game with the same people. Instead they gave me the chance to notice things I never noticed before, and I learned a lot, and that's what a sports camp's for, right?

But I didn't think a second week would teach me much more.

irst we decided if I worked my tail off that first week and impressed *every* assistant and the skating lady and Marco, they'd tell my dad not to bother sending me a second week. So I did that. But one day I passed the office and heard Marco and the lady talking about some papers they were both looking at and I hung outside long enough to hear they were worried about enrollment being down for the next week. I told Dooby.

"You're toast, then, as far as getting them to rec-ommend a reprieve," he said. "Marco likes to keep those spots filled, at three hundred dollars a week. If necessary, he'll tell your dad you've done nothing but skate half-speed and shoot slapshots into the glass when you should have been watching him demonstrate something, and knock down every cone in drills. We better think of something else."

"I hate to sound redundant," said Zip, "but we

could arrange for Billy's father to meet with a particularly unpleasant accident of some sort—"

"Hey—"

"Come on, Zip," said Woodsie. "He's only kidding, Billy." He studied me for a minute. "What happens if you say 'No, Dad'?"

"If I say *what*?"

"Never mind," Woodsie said.

"It's Wednesday," Barry said. "How about if you go home tonight, and say, oh, like, you know, you've done more than half a week, worked hard, and camp, like, isn't challenging, isn't rough enough, really sucks in fact, and you hate it? You're very much afraid it's likely to start interfering, messing up your 'natural ability' and making you, like, *hesitant*—unsure of your instincts? He seems like the kind of guy who likes instincts over studyin'."

I said, "He'll just find somewhere to get me a *third* week where I can play wild and put it all together."

Woodsie said, "There's that weird football thing, you know, the mechanical tendency to reduce everything to very precisely rehearsed steps.

Football players *crave* directions. So maybe he won't be as anti-study as you think."

"Hmm."

Zip said, "Look, he hates *us*, right? How about if we convince him somehow that *we* are the perfect representatives of Marco's camp and coaching philosophy?"

"That might work if Marco's team last year hadn't won forty more games than we did."

"Point," said Zip. "And by the way it wasn't the goaltending."

We went through the hour of power skating and it hurt, not as bad as the first day, but the knowledge that I might be doing this next week while the guys were body surfing and scarfing the crabs made me feel twice as bad. We did the drills and I nailed them. Then, surprise, my dad showed up for the scrimmage.

The Wings held a quick conference. "Does Billy suck, or play great?" Dooby asked.

"Well, if he sucks, he needs another week worse than ever," said Barry.

"But if he plays great, it's just a measure of Marco's excellence and bodes especially well for that extra week's bit of edge," said Woodsie.

"*I* know," I said. They all looked at me.

"I can play soft," I said. "He'll hate *that*."

"No way," said Zip. "He'll get Marco alone in that office and make him watch his punt-return highlight film until Marco has us all killing each other out here. *And* chasing each other's helmets."

As it was, I played the way I was learning, and I looked good, scored a goal, assisted on two, covered the ice, skated pretty. There's no denying it's a good camp. There's no denying I'm a pretty decent player, either.

My dad was pleased. On the way home he chuckled and said, "Can't wait till those *chumps* leave, and you sneak back on 'em and get in some extra work and pull off into the sunset while they eat some ice shavings." My heart sagged.

here's twenty-one bedrooms," said Zip.

"No way!"

Zip nodded. "My great-grandfather was a nut. Every time he invited someone to visit he built a new room for him, he had a thing about using them—rooms—for more than one person, like they were underwear or something. So the place is, like, a shaggy clapboard castle sort of deal. *Way* high. If we wanted we could invite the whole team, but we like it to be, you know, kind of a *special* thing." He sucked on the straw of his root beer.

He didn't need to make it sound any better— a huge old house hanging onto the top of a sand dune looking straight down at the sea, full of good food and stuff, but most of all, filled with—the guys! Frankly, I wouldn't have expected it—it was like a gift or something. *What about Prince? I wanted to ask. Surely you like him better than me!*

What about Shinny? Ernie? Boot?

But they picked me.

"After a week of being pinched and cold inside these nasty ice skates, boy, I tell you, your feet spread out into that warm sand. . . ." Dooby closed his eyes and smiled.

I thought about more cones.

They kept going. The sun, the waves, the fishing, the walks at night on the beach when you could tell the shapes of girls way up ahead in the dark by, well, by *shape*. . . .

And then all of a sudden they maybe went a little too far. All of a sudden I found myself starting to wonder if maybe my dad wasn't a little bit correct. They *did* start to sound like a bunch of goof-offs who couldn't wait to shed the nuisance of hockey and just hit the surf. I thought back to the season, to how some of those 14–1 losses felt. They sucked, that's how they felt. I never wanted to lose 14–1 again, certainly not like all the time.

Would a week of extra camp make the difference?

I knew what my dad hoped. He wanted me to leave the Wings and make the AA Little Caps team, a very elite team directly sponsored by the local

NHL team, with fancy leather jackets and free season tickets to the (Big) Caps games, and some of their *seventy-five* regular season games even broadcast on cable. I had tried out the year before, and got cut in the last bunch of about six kids. My dad liked to tell people I was the "last one let go"—the coach hated to do it, really wanted to keep me, all that stuff. It's more like I was just in a bunch of six or seven kids, and I frankly knew I had no business playing with the ones who made it, not even close, they were awesome, they deserved their jackets and cable broadcasts. My dad hadn't brought the Little Caps up again yet, but I knew that's where his hopes were. The last thing in the world he would want is me spreading my toes out in the warm sand and talking about dirty books with Dooby and Zip (both of whom had older brothers and hinted strongly that the beach house held quite a thrilling secret library. . . .)

Okay, I told myself: think about it for a minute. Maybe I *could* make the Little Caps.

Did I *want* to? Seventy-five regular season games?

My dad would be pretty pumped—I pictured

the first time I walked out in my leather jacket.

But what if I just *barely* made the team, and hardly played? Or got humiliated when I *was* on the ice, because like the only reason I made the team was one lousy extra week of Marco's camp, which I already knew wasn't going to exactly transform my game?

Did I owe it to my dad to try?

I sure didn't owe it to him to flop at the beach with a bunch of kids he didn't respect, kids who had already shown they knew how to lose bigtime.

Then, I told myself, think about *not* making the Little Caps. Then I was a Wing again! But—I was a Wing who missed out on the good times that made everybody hang close. I was a Wing who chose to push the serious hockey thing instead of making buds, which is important, and yet I knew I could never convince my dad it really mattered, not with these guys especially, he had already chucked these guys in the Dumpster.

I could hear him say something like, "You want friends? There's plenty of nice kids out there who know how to poke check and shoot backhand. Being good doesn't make them unreachable. *Those* are your people, Billy. Get your talent together and go find them."

But Dooby and Cody were already here.

And I liked them.

And I liked being about as good as I was on the Wings, or as good as I would be, which would probably be in the top six or seven or eight. Maybe I didn't want to be number one.

eight

Thursday morning Dooby took one look at me and could tell something had happened. "What is it?" he said to me, for a second looking serious and concerned so that I almost busted out bawling but then I remembered, *Hey, it's Doobs, don't be silly, you bozo.*

I reached in a side pocket of my hockey bag and pulled out a bunch of papers and handed them to him. He read a few, then flipped through the rest. Then he put his hand on my shoulder for just a second. Zip walked up at that moment and said, "Am I in time for the kiss?"

Dooby looked at him and rustled the papers. "Billy's dad's nocturnal emission," he said. "A son, skating pretty, on the Little Caps."

"Oooh, leather," said Zip, reaching for the application and recommendation stuff my father had given me that morning to give Marco and the lady. He did about the same amount of reading, then looked at me.

"You good enough?"

I hesitated, but shook my head. "No way I can see."

"Then no prob," Zip said, and before I could stop him he ripped the papers *snarp* across the middle and then ripped them again.

"What—!"

He stuffed them back into my bag pocket roughly. "Marco and his lads and ladies just expressed their opinion. Not even your dad can miss the innuendo. Those pages are in *eighths* now."

"He'll call them!" I yelled, my voice cracking. "You don't know him! He won't—he won't—" I kind of fluttered.

Woodsie had walked up. "He won't take 'No' for an answer? That's what you were going to say." He punched me on the shoulder. "Let me ask you something: how do you know he won't? Has he ever heard 'No' for an answer, Billy?"

"He's, he's, like, a confident guy, you don't understand—"

"Excuse me, but actually he's more of a bully,"

said Dooby. "The only confidence he has is what he borrows from *your* talent."

"Bully," I said.

Woodsie nodded like all somber and final. "And you know what you have to do with a bully."

"Whatever he wants, right?" said Zip with a straight face, and it *did* sound so stupid I barked out a stupid laugh, and started crying for about two seconds at the same moment.

Dooby waggled my shoulders. "Hey, hey," he said. "Remember—you're not in this alone, right?"

"He also said you couldn't play for the Wings again, didn't he?" said Woodsie.

I nodded.

"What a total—"

"We've got to think pretty fast," Dooby said, rubbing his chin. "This is going to take a little subtlety, I'm afraid."

"What a waste," said Zip.

"Look," I said, spinning on him, feeling my face go hot, "he hates you, too, okay? And he didn't lose twenty-nine games last season, either."

There was a moment of kind of stunned silence, then Woodsie said, "Exactly."

"What do you mean?" I snapped.

Woodsie shrugged. "Pardon me for pointing it out—but what has *he* put on the line? What dues has *he* paid, you know? I mean, he has no trouble judging the Wings as losers—all the way, personally as well as athletically—but *he* wasn't out there fighting every single loss." He shrugged. "It's easy to talk about a team with a massively bad record as if it, like, all happened at once, as a kind of verdict or something. But we played last season game by game, for *six months*. Pass by pass. Up and down the ice, up and down, watch the trailer, poke the puck, block that lane to the goal. We got beat, in those *little* battles, but who knows? It *could* turn out different. And even if it doesn't, we'll still have to fight for every single advantage, block every single threat. Shift by shift." He jabbed himself in the chest. "*Us*. The *players*. On the *ice*."

I was shaking my head. Dooby said, "Hey, let me ask you, Billy—are *you* a loser?" Before I could answer he said, "Of course not! You're exempt, right? You—you're not one of those pukey Wing losers, you're *special*, you're talent, you're going to make the Little Caps and leave the rest of us riff-raff bunched together." Dooby poked me softly in the shoulder. "But you were there, too, weren't you, Bill? How does he figure out a way to get around that? And, what's more, you want to go to the beach too, just like the rest of us, because it's *summer*, man, and you're a *kid*, remember?, instead of pretending a week of skating more grim swivels is going to separate you surgically from the lepers."

Woodsie smacked himself in the forehead. We all looked at him. "We keep telling Billy we're going to help him. But seems we're leaving out an awful lot we ought to do," he said, and looked at Zip. "Technically, shouldn't your mother be the one to suggest that Billy come along for the beach week?"

"Yeah, I guess, I mean she usually, you know, as kind of a formality, but—"

"Yeah," said Woodsie, nodding slowly. "Well, it's formality time, and high time, too."

I shook my head. "Won't matter. She calls today, he'll blow her away."

Woodsie looked shocked. "Surely he wouldn't, like, you know"—he gestured helplessly—"call us, like, bad company, or losers and so on, to Zip's mom—"

"He'd just say I was occupied. Over and out. Thank you very much."

"Ah." They thought. "Well," said Cody, "it's worth a try."

"I don't know," I said. "Once he smells this beach-trip rat—"

"What can he do? Chain you to your bed? Don't answer that," said Zip.

"Should one of *us* ask him?"

"Oh, sure."

"Just checking."

Woodsie nodded at the shreds sticking out of my bag. "Do you know if that's, like, his first approach to Marco, about the Little Caps certainly, but maybe about next week too?"

I thought. "I don't know."

"Have you delivered anything else to Marco?"

"No."

They nodded, and Dooby said, "Good."

"Why?"

Woodsie said, "Marco ain't cashed the check yet for next week, we got more room to maneuver."

A whistle blew. "Look," I said. "I appreciate all this and all, but, like, it comes down to me, doesn't it? And, like, he's my dad, and I can't help it, and I know I won't just stand there in his face and say 'Forget it, Dude,' okay?"

"Sure," said Zip, giving my forehead a quick rub, "sure, that's okay. If that's how it works out. Just hold out as long as you can, okay?"

I nodded. Second whistle. Ice time.

Today I noticed for the first time that the lady's skating drills kind of hooked together. The first ones were painfully slow and used only your feet, then the next ones worked in your ankles, and the next ones got your knees involved, all in unison. Then you started over, only alternating feet, ankles, knees. Then you brought more leg into it, then hips, and finally you were using everything from the waist down, finally using it *hard*. But still above the waist you were squared off frontways, motionless, head up, both hands on your stick, blade on the ice in front of you. Now that I had noticed this was how we ended up, I tried to keep it pretty much that way when we started free skating and when the pucks came out and we began to stickhandle. And it dawned on me, if I stayed calm and still upstairs and got all my power going downstairs, I had all kinds of extra control and vision.

As if she was reading my mind, the lady—her name was just Jane to us—came right by me and popped me on the back of the helmet and said, "Day breaks for another disgruntled victim of meaningless torture."

"I get it, I think!" I said.

"I know!" she said back over her shoulder as she skated away. "You're supposed to get it, sometime!"

I drilled that way, letting myself get a little more flexible, and the advantage stayed. I was skating from the feet to the hips, and the rest of me was free to do whatever it needed to do. The drills went the best they had. I even drew a couple of whistles from guys for flashy tight turns with the puck around cones.

At lunch, Zip said, "My mom's calling."

That day we did a double-length scrimmage after lunch. It was just what I needed, a chance to like try consciously what my body had probably been trying to get me to try unconsciously all week. First time I got the puck I was skating back for it into our zone and I made a big half-circle and took it out up the far boards, which squared me off against this Montrose center skating backwards.

Now, when you skate backwards you are naturally squared up, at least until you have to move to the side. Then you either have to slant or, if you want to face up still, you have to cross over backwards. Get a guy to cross over backwards and if you time it right you can blow by him to the other side and he's helpless, he can't come out of the move without breaking his legs. I blew by the Montrose center just over the red line. A defenseman had cruised over to keep me to the outside, though, so I wasn't loose. I noticed that when he moved my way he left Cody and Cody wasn't going full speed yet so I snapped a pass ahead of him, onside, perfect against the path of the defenseman. Just like that, Cody was streaking down the slot. The other D had to come over to take him, and Cody flipped a backhand pass over his stick blade to this kid named Jeremy from Easton and he stuffed it.

"Sheeze," said the defenseman who had come over to cover me, tapping his stick against the ice. "That was so *easy*, wasn't it? How come it never seems like it's *always* that easy?"

"It's camp. We're not killing ourselves to stop everything," I said.

"Speak for yourself," he said. "I'm trying to get Marco to think I'm the next Chelios and take me on his Montrose A's."

"Ah," I said. That hadn't occurred to me—that this was kind of a chance to show off for the great Marco and impress him and make *his* team. A cold thought hit me. Surely *that* wasn't—but, no. My dad was still thinking Little Caps. But maybe his idea of a fallback was—jeez—*Montrose*. I shuddered, right there on the ice. Being friendly in camp was okay and all, but surely nobody could ever expect a Wing . . .

I intercepted a pass off the face-off and looked up quick and saw nobody up ahead, and noticed at the same time that my hips were angled ahead of *both* of the guys who were supposed to stay between me and the goalie. So I just took off. Sure enough, neither could catch me—amazing isn't it?—a little advantage of position and you can make it into something, and I did. I froze the goalie with my loosey-goosey upper-body freedom, shaking shoulders and stuff until he just watched, barely interested while I snapped the puck into the near corner. True, I did not pass, just like before; true, I took it all the way in myself, like then; but *this* time I had checked and *then* done the right thing, and I knew it and so did my teammates. They all rubbed me up and swatted me and barked and stuff and really meant it—it *was* a pretty goal, it *was* nice skating.

For my last two shifts, the assistant dude coaching my team against Marco's put me at defenseman. When he told me the first time I said, "I never did it. I got no idea."

He didn't seem too worried. "Play as if it was against yourself with the puck," he said, "only *stop* yourself. And maybe anticipate more and wait for developments less."

The first time a guy skated at me with the puck I stopped and faced him at the *first* blue line and took a weak swing at it and then turned and watched as he vanished into a three-on-two that scored. The second time a guy came at me I at least waited until the red line to let him whiz past. But from then on I stopped turning and stopping—I skated forward as long as I could keep the guy wide, and swiveled and skated backwards *hard* only in my zone. That worked better. I took one shot from the point. It was blocked by somebody's skate thirty feet from the cage. When you stand out there at the point and look in at the net it seems amazing any shot ever gets through all that mess and still has the zip to pop by the goalie—it's like it surely has to twist and turn and wind its way to get there.

My father showed for just those last two shifts and I could tell with just a couple of glances that he was not exactly happy with me playing D. He was muttering to himself and shaking his head and never met my eyes at all, even when I corrected my first couple of humiliating fizzles.

Then I remembered. Maybe it wasn't the scrimmage that had him upset. Maybe Zip's mom had called and asked me down to the beach. For some reason, I just knew that would make him cranky, like he was acting. More cranky than me scrimmaging out of position.

I blocked a shot with ten seconds left and decided to kill the clock by rushing the puck up myself, a little Bobby Orr action, end-to-end excitment. But I got poke-checked from behind with seven seconds left, and that was plenty of time for the other guys to turn it around and leave me at the red line and pass back and forth until they found my man open and he scored at the buzzer. So much for being an offensive flash.

On the way home my dad said nothing. Not one thing. He just pulled his lip and looked like he wasn't concerned about much, certainly not the hockey player sitting a foot away.

fter dinner my dad, still without like looking at me a single time or saying anything, pushed himself up from the table and said, "Let's talk," to the air above his plate. I followed him into the den, where all his football stuff is, where I always felt pretty much nothing but pride in him but something else a little too, and this time that thing was *all* I felt: intimidation.

He plopped into his soft chair and held out his hand. After a second or two he snapped his fingers once, and said, "The recommendations. I want to see what Marco has to say so far."

I was not going to hand him Zip's ripped-up copy, so I just said, "I gave it to him and he looked at it for a second then looked at me like I was dreaming or something, then frowned and stuck it under his arm and went on to the next thing with somebody else." I think it was the first time I ever lied to my dad. It came pretty easy but it felt bad. Still, I added some extra detail. "I like got the feeling he didn't take it real seriously, really. Like, not a joke maybe, but—" I shrugged.

Blam! My father shocked me by smacking the arm of his chair with the flat of his hand *hard*, and saying a pretty nasty word in a very nasty way. He was maybe angrier than I ever saw him, if that's what it was, anger. He said the word again, more under control, then looked at me for the first time.

"You know what that probably means?"

I said, "No extra help for the Little Caps?"

My dad laughed sarcastically and shook his head and rolled his eyes once. "I think you can probably forget the Little Caps," he said. "But"—he couldn't decide whether to cuss again or sigh and he finally chose the sigh—"this sends a pretty clear message about Montrose."

"Montrose?"

"Montrose?" he repeated in my dumb way, leaving his mouth hanging open. Then he sighed again and shook his head. "I figured the Little Caps were a long shot but I hoped at least you'd manage to impress him enough to get into his thoughts about his own team."

"You thought I'd play for Montrose?"

"You should be so lucky, I guess," he said. Then he shot me a dark look and pointed his finger at my head. "And, please, spare me any oh-I-couldn't-possibly-I'm-too-loyal-to-dear-old-Wolfbay stuff. If you could get on that Montrose team—if there was *any* way, and there still might be, still might—you ought to fall down dead in gratitude."

I let a lot of stuff and a lot of time pass, kind of dropping my chin on my chest, and finally just said, "I guess I didn't make much of an impression. And I've been playing hot, too."

"Spare me," he said. "I can't help taking Marco's apparent conclusion as representing your 'heat' a little more accurately." He heaved a sigh. "Well," he said, digging something—his checkbook—out of his back pocket, uncapping a pen, and writing a check as he talked, "this just makes next week all the more crucial. It's *key*. Here." He held out the check. I took a couple of steps and pinched it by the edge.

He pointed again. "You give that to Marco—personally, into his hand, with as much eagerness as you can put into it—you give that to him first thing." He leaned back. "Least he'll know you're coming next week before any more damage gets done."

I swallowed a couple of times. "Dad?"

"What?"

"I, um, like don't think, like, that it's, that I'll, you know, be *that* different, I mean that impressive all of a sudden, just repeating the same exact stuff, it's not like I'm going to get *awesome* at cone drills all of a sudden or—"

"What does that have to do with anything?" He was holding both hands out, palms up, as if totally like mystified by my comment.

"I assume you want me to have the extra week as like extra time to display—"

"Display," he said with a quick laugh. "Hey, you can relax, okay? Don't break your neck trying to cut a half-second off your circle-drills. *That*'s not why you're going to be there next week." He looked at me incredulously. "Surely you understand *that*?"

I could just shake my head.

"All right, Billy. Try very, very hard to concentrate, okay? You are not taking the extra week because I expect you to show *squat* to Marco, as far as ability goes. You are taking the extra week—and the fact that it never occurred to you shows all too well how little of these things, these qualities, you actually *feel*, which disappoints me plenty, Buster—you are taking the week only, *only*, to demonstrate your seriousness about hockey, your determination to do *everything* to improve *any* aspect of your game, your *devotion* and *single-mindedness* and your special difference from all of the other bozos who will be heading for the—*beach*." He spat the last word.

I swallowed. "Oh," I said.

He looked at me for a long time. "You'd probably rather join them, am I right? You'd probably like to put on the old Jams and hang loose with the dudes, huh? And especially since you've been actually *invited* to chuck your week away in the *perfect* company."

"The beach isn't so bad, is it?" I said. "I mean, you know, it's, like, fun and stuff, and if you're also with your teammates—"

"*Those people are not your teammates.*" He glared me down. "Do you understand, Billy? You will never play on a team with Zip and good ol' *Doobs* and all the rest *ever again*. They are *losers*. Or weren't you watching last year?"

"No," I said. "I wasn't. I wasn't watching."

This answer surprised him, so I kept going. "I wasn't watching us *lose*. I was out there playing, you know? *Trying*? Trying *hard*? Like all of those guys. You call them—you call *us*—all losers, but we went out onto the ice at the start of every game and tried to win. We didn't look ahead and say, 'Oh, I foresee this will be another eight-goal loss.' Every goal against us—every *one*, was, like, a terrible surprise, a sudden pain like getting stabbed, that wasted all this work we'd been doing."

He said calmly, "And you'd say working so hard to achieve a 9–29–5 record was an efficient use of your time and talent? You'd gladly repeat the"—he smiled a little to himself but it was for me to see— "the *effort*?"

"You bet," I said. "I'd repeat the *effort* any day. I wouldn't mind a few new players with tons of talent too, but that's *all* I would change. The record? That would, like, change by itself, or not, depending on what kind of talent we had and what we faced."

"Something wrong with Montrose's talent? Or record?"

"You really think Marco's going to be so impressed with my one extra week of dedication he'll just stick me right in there beside Kenny Moseby and let me mop up all those assists?"

He just stared.

I felt all my energy fading fast. "I just want to have fun," I said. "And, yes—I *did*, I had *fun* last year. And these guys do not hate me and they're not jealous either. They're just good guys. And the beach is just the beach, and it's fun too."

He stared at me for another few minutes. Then he pushed himself up with a grunt and walked out past me without another look.

"Just give Marco that check," he said as he left. "First thing. In his hand."

I sat for a minute in the room, with its trophies and pictures and that helmet my dad chased down after his big hit. "Kenny Moseby," I said, putting the check in my pocket, "Kenny Moseby, maybe your lucky day is just about to come. But I doubt it, Kenny, old buddy."

didn't exactly give the check to Zip, not exactly, but I told him about it and I knew he would take it right away. He did, but he did not tear it up, he put it in a space beneath his blocker pad, like between it and the back of the glove, very careful to keep it flat, and very serious too. I did not know what he might do, I had no idea.

When the four of them came over this morning they had a present for me, a real one, in a box, wrapped in red paper, no ribbon but I did not care.

"Shut up and don't say thanks, just open it," Dooby said before I could say anything at all. So I did, sitting there with my lowers on but no shoulder pads or skates or anything. I opened my present, just like that.

It was a pair of very baggy Jams. They had a black background, and the design over that was dozens of silhouettes, silver, of that same girl sitting and leaning back on her arms with one leg drawn up and one stretched out that truck drivers put chrome cutouts of on their black rubber mudflaps. You see her everywhere like that. She has a lot of long hair, too. I guess she is what they dream about.

"I had them in red," Cody said. "These are way better."

"*Way* better," Dooby agreed. "Plus you were only seven years old and still very cute, and you looked really stupid with pornographic lowlife Jams on."

"Don't worry," Woodsie said to me. "Even though you are younger than we are you have passed the point of being cute. They will look righteous on you, though of course still pornographic and extremely lowlife, much more lowlife than in red."

"That summer I remember what Zip and Dooby wore—they both had these suits with Ninja Turtles on them," said Cody. "So—I mean, get serious—who was cooler?"

I take my hockey pants off and easily slip the Jams on over my socks and drawers, then put the hockey pants back on.

"That was pretty cool," says Dooby.

"Now I feel nice and dirty," I said.

"You don't even know what 'dirty' means," Woodsie says. "But we'll let you get away with it."

"At least I never wore a bathing suit with a Ninja Turtle on it," I said. "So I must know *something*."

It's Friday, last day of the week camp, and everybody who usually acts tough with us is acting silly and there's like a celebration feeling on the ice. We do the skating but it seems easy and even fun, we do the cones and stuff, we eat lunch, and then, as a treat, we get back on the ice for more than a double scrimmage session. We are going to finish strong, by playing hockey until we flop.

I am put on a line scheduled for the third shift of the game. During the second shift, I see my father walk into the spectator area, across the rink behind the glass. I tried to read his expression. There wasn't much of one.

On my first shift I lost the puck three times in a row without even being challenged. Then in the middle of the shift I heard a couple of yells and snuck a look across the rink at my dad and was completely surprised to see Zip, in his full equipment and carrying a normal stick as well as his goalie stick, skating over to Marco and explaining something. Then Zip skated to the opening in the boards closest to where my dad was standing. While I watched, Zip banged on the glass with his own stick until the gate was opened, and he made an obvious gesture for my dad to come over and talk to him.

I didn't want to, but I figured I'd better skate over. But Dooby, who was on the ice too, stopped me after two strides.

"Let Zip," he said.

"Let him do what?"

"Help things a little," Dooby said. "Besides, it's more about Zip and all of us than about you, anyway." By this point my father had turned very red and come over to where Zip stood at the gate. I couldn't hear what they were saying but it was clear they weren't exactly hiding their feelings. Zip was making big gestures and my father was too, and looking very sarcastic. I was stunned then to see Zip remove his catching glove and with his bare hand remove the check I was supposed to give to Marco that morning. He waved it at my father.

My father actually made a lunge for it with one hand, but Zip was too quick, and backskated about eight feet. My father was furious now, but he listened as Zip explained something. Then, to my complete shock, my dad, in his street shoes, stepped carefully out onto the ice, and took the hockey stick Zip now offered him. They both turned toward the goal Zip had been defending and Zip offered my father his arm to balance on but my dad would die first. Zip stopped briefly when they were passing Marco, who was on the ice to ref the scrimmage. Zip explained something to him, and handed him the folded check, which Marco, frowning but looking kind of curious and amused too, took and held between his fingers, like he was being the neutral party in a bet.

Which he was. When my father got near Zip's goal I saw something really weird. Somehow, while the action was down at the other end, Zip had managed to set up eight pucks in a perfect semi-circle about eight feet out from his cage. My father stopped by one of these, and looked at Zip, who was talking. As if to make it clear to everybody, Zip, before putting his catching glove back on, held up his index finger for a couple of moments.

Dooby said, "He's telling him that if he gets just one by him—"

"I got the idea," I said. "And if Zip stones him—"

"Then I guess it's time to pack the sunscreen and boogie board."

My father was silent now, and serious, all concentration. He was holding the stick but he was still upright, not bending down yet to take a whack at any one of the pucks. Zip meanwhile snapped into his tight goalie's position like they do for face-offs. He was playing pretty deep in his net. Frankly, I would have bet on my dad. I had the feeling Dooby felt the same way, was maybe a little worried.

The whole place was silent. Everyone watched my dad. And you know what? He looked pretty brave out there even though he was still very large and very quietly angry, holding some stranger's stick that was too short, in his black leather tie shoes on the white ice, facing a goaltender in full gear, all set for his sneakiest shot.

He slipped his left hand down the shaft, and

bent over, and lined up the puck that was third in from the left.

"He scores," I said. "He scores by the fourth shot. My dad's an athlete." It sounded like I was almost rooting for him.

But we will never know if he would have put one past Zip. Because before taking any kind of shot, my father looked until he located me. He locked my eyes and said, "What do you think, Billy?"

"You'll beat him," I said.

He was still bent over. "But do I shoot?" I blinked, so he explained. "Does it make any difference?"

"No," I said. "Even if you win, I'm going to the beach."

"Well, then," he said, and straightened up, shook his head, flipped the stick to the ice, and turned to walk back to the gate, head high, looking straight ahead. Zip stayed where he was. Everyone was whispering now.

Just after he passed Marco my dad doubled back and held out his hand. Marco gave him the check he had been holding in his fingertips the same way the whole time. My father neatly tore it into bits and let them flutter to the ice. Then he turned and walked through the gate in the boards, through the crowd that parted for him, and out the door to the warm room.

I looked down at Zip. He looked at me too. Despite his glove and blocker pad and stick, he managed to use both of his arms and imitate a swimming motion. I nodded. Then I turned to Dooby. "I've got to go catch my dad."

Dooby nodded, frowning slightly, distracted. "Why didn't he shoot?"

"He talks a lot about pride," I said. "Maybe that was it, just then. Either that, or Zip scared the crap out of him."

Kind of hopping on my skates I broke through into the warm room just as he was going through the far doors to the parking lot.

"Hey, Dad!" I called, stopping.

He turned and looked at me over his shoulder. He thought for a second, and turned back to the door. "I'll be in the car," he said.

While I changed I heard the scrimmage get going again just like normal but with that little extra happy-Friday-last-day thing, and it hit me I could feel it too now and I did. It had been a big week and it was over and now I was going to the beach to get loose, to make friends, and even though my dad didn't know it, wouldn't believe it, to make the hockey team better too, probably. Thinking of him made me think I ought not to be enjoying the idea of the beach. I wasn't sure what happened inside him out there, I wasn't sure I would ever know or understand how bad, or how good, or how high or low, how cruel or how just. So I let it go at least for the moment.

But as I walked up to the car and he popped the trunk and I threw my junk in and slammed it and walked around to my door—

"He ought to be president of these United States," my father said before I even got the door all the way open. He was sitting behind the wheel with his arms crossed and I saw his ankles were crossed too, which meant he was just *sitting*, he wasn't *driving*, and he was relaxed. As I sat and settled he chuckled and shook his head. "President. For life. Fix things *right* up, no doubt about it, let all those wimpy overseas dependents know what's what, yank a knot in the tail here at home."

"You talking about Zip, Dad?"

"Balls of steel, is what I am talking about. Balls of *diamond*." He laughed again, and took a look at me. It was a nice look, the nicest from him in a long time, I realized. "And willing to put them on the line for a person who means something to him, which I cannot help but respect."

"Zip's pretty cool," I said.

"I didn't realize," he said, still looking at me. "Had no idea. Couldn't see it. It just did not occur to me that those boys *took you in* like that. I mean— loyalty, taking a punch, whatever, the fact is, they *like* you, they *want* you to stick with them, they have put you on their team and they do not intend to give you up easy."

I'm sure you should be like humiliated and angry and hurt when your dad tells you he could not imagine your friends actually *caring* about you, but it wasn't worth it. And I suppose you would wish the new respect you saw in his face was in-spired by something you did, more than what somebody else was like moved to do *for* you, but it belongs to you anyway, you earned it *somehow*, and so you just take it.

"I guess I'm an okay guy if I get a lot of slack," I said.

"You're a lot better than *that*, Billy, and you deserve a lot more respect, or at least a different kind, than you've been getting from a certain close male relative who got his ass handed to him in a sling by a twelve-year-old today for being so dense."

"I was betting you would have scored," I said. "I was ready to get the skates sharpened for another week. I *knew* you were going to put one by him."

"Then it's *really* a good thing I didn't shoot," he said. "By the way, let's see the Jams."

"He told you about the *Jams*?" I said.

"He's what you call a 'communicator,'" my dad said. "You spend two or three minutes with him and you *know* some stuff, from the details to the principles."

"I'm wearing them," I said.

"Then spare me. So, okay, you're set for a dirty swimsuit. What else do you need?"

"What? Like, you mean, for the beach?"

He had uncrossed his ankles and was reaching for the key in the ignition. "Sandals, suntan lotion, Frisbees, I don't know. What? Think about it. We'll

head downtown and get whatever you want to take.
Within reason. I might stretch it to one of those little belly-board things but don't ask for a surfboard
just yet. I *do* have my pride."

He started the car and we went.

Here's a sneak peek at the next book in the
Wolfbay Wings ice hockey
series by Bruce Brooks

available from HarperCollins

As I walked into the locker room on the first day of hockey practice, my very first day as a Peewee, which is the stupid name for the next level up from the even more stupidly designated Squirts, I could not help noticing something that had nothing to do with hockey. You know how it is—when you're curious, you can't help picking up signals from anything that seems to be sending them.

Well, that first day, when my antennae were fully extended and I was taking readings on whatever I could, I noticed—first thing, without trying— that some of these very mature fellows who so proudly called themselves Peewees seemed to believe they needed to *shave*. Because there, standing over a sink in front of a mirror, contorting a face covered with white foam and preparing to scrape it with a razor I could only assume was loaded with a genuine lethally sharp metal blade, was a second year Peewee named Sandy Beckstein, who was, at the very most, barely twelve years old and whose skin was almost certainly as hairless as mine.

—What're you doing? I asked Sandy at just the moment he started an upstroke along his neck. He jumped a little, and, as I had hoped, sure enough, some blood started to discolor his foam.

His eyes looked for mine in the mirror and found them. I'm practicing my backhand, Dork-breath, he said. Then he lifted his razor, which looked like a raygun from an old space movie, and actually did swipe it across his cheek back-handed.

—Nice, I said. Now let's see you stickhandle.

But before Sandy could figure out how to respond to that, Pincher Greene, another of last year's Peewees, spoke up very loudly from a bench.

—Quiet! Here comes—just another hockey player!

The door opened and a girl dressed in a Wings practice sweater and the rest of the hockey equipment walked in.

I looked at her, then over at Cody, generally a modest guy, who had everything off but his cup pants, and Zip, far from modest, who had every-thing off but his jock.

Zip smiled warmly at the girl and with one thumb held the waistband of his jock three inches out from his stomach.

—Quarter for a peek, he said.

The girl, who had not returned his smile, dumped her bag on the floor, took a bored look at Zip, and sat down on the bench.

—Nope, she said. You'd have to pay me at least a buck to look in there.

—I meant—

—She knows what you meant, puckhead, said Cody. She made a funny.

—Oh, said Zip. I get it. Instead of her paying— oh, ho ho.

—I thought it was pretty good, Cody said.

—Then you get to center her line, said Pincher.

—I probably will, said Cody. Is she any good?

—*That* will cost more than a quarter to find out, said Pincher.

—I meant—

But the girl waved Cody quiet and said, I know what you meant, and the answer, *free*, is that I am not very good *but* I would appreciate you letting this guy keep building up his large inventory of primitive innuendos, because the Supreme Court will be putting him away for a long time any day now. She looked at the rest of us. See, it is illegal for you to notice that I am gender-differentiated from you he-men. In fact, as the boys here will help me tell you on three, I am—one, two, and-uh-three—

—*Just another hockey player*, hollered Sandy and Pincher and the girl.

—So, Peewee teammates! I said, rubbing my hands. We Peewees shave, and we share our locker room with gender-undifferentiated girls—but is there any *real* difference from Squirts?

—Yeah, said Sandy. By now he had scraped most of his foam off. Yeah: Up here we don't lose twenty-nine games.

—We'll just see about *that*, I said with a chuckle. There's a fresh new wind blowin' into this team, and it's capable of sweeping—

—Do you always talk this much? the girl asked me.

—Always, said Woodsie as he walked through the door.

—So you *didn't* take that scholarship to the quantum mechanics lab at MIT after all! I said to him.

—Who are you? Pincher asked him.

—He's the Duke of Earl, said Cody.

—The Sultan of Swat, said Zip.

—The Pause That Refreshes, said Woodsie.

—His name is Woods and he is going to take your job, Beckstein said as he felt up and down his throat.

Pincher is a defenseman who skates very pretty and thus always makes travel teams. But he has one bad habit, and it is enough to make him almost useless. When a defenseman chooses not to hold his point position or to backskate once the other guys have taken possession of the puck, but instead chases the puck *into* his offensive zone, he is said to be "pinching." Pinching usually results in the other guys' skating by the defenseman in a whoosh and getting a two-on-one the other way. As you might gather from his name, Pincher finds it impossible not to leave his post and chase after the puck whenever it comes within fifteen feet of him. He rarely gets it. Goalies, who tend to fare poorly against two-on-ones, despise him, as do many coaches. But he does skate so pretty . . .

—Are you really a defenseman? he asked Woodsie, and Woodsie nodded. Pincher groaned and uttered a very bad word.

—What did you expect, Pinch? I said. Did you think the Squirts didn't have any defensemen or something?

—Well, he said through his sulk, you *did* lose a million games.

—It was the goaltending and the goaltending alone, said Cody.

—Here's another one, Beckstein said as Barry shuffled in. And *he's* better than you are too, Pinch, *way* better.

—Are you? Pinch asked.

—Am I what? Barry said cautiously.

—A better defenseman than I am.

—Oh, said Barry, unslinging his bag and letting it fall. Oh, def.

Pinch said another bad word and added, How many D are you guys bringing up, anyway?

—Jeez, why don't you whine or something? said the girl.

—Why don't *you* grow a goatee? Pinch snapped.

—Now, boys! I said. And of course, ladies—

—First of all, there isn't but one of me, so keep it singular, and second, remember that the Supreme Court is all set to jump all over your tail and ruin the rest of your life: phone taps, twenty-four-hour surveillance, saltpeter in your food . . .

—Sorry, I said. But what *do* I call you?

—Hey, said Barry, noticing her for the first time and gaping.

—Careful, she said to him. Under certain statutes, staring may be interpreted as a form of sexual harassment. To me she said, You may call me Nathan.

—Nathan.

—For half the season last year her daddums had to come in here and hand her each piece of equipment to make sure she got it on just right, Pincher said in an ugly voice.

—My father is a dip, she said with a sigh. He is unconvinced that I can breathe unless he is here to contribute the influence of his male knowledge of the universe's mechanics.

—How did you get rid of him? I asked.

—The boys came up with the very sophisticated technique of engaging in an endless relay of mouth-farts, she said. It finally drove him away.

—You should have heard us, Pincher laughed. We were awesome. He issued a fairly decent mouth-fart to demonstrate, but no one, not even Beckstein, followed up.

—Why Nathan? I asked her.

She shrugged. It's about as far as you can get from Kathy, she said, which is my gender-differen-tiated name.

—Did the others call you Nathan in front of your father? Woodsie asked.

—Oh, certainly, she said. He thought they were referring to someone else, a player he never managed to identify all year, even though he kept statistics on the entire team.

—Oh, no, said Zip. Not one of *those* fathers.

—I'm afraid so, she said. But don't worry. He only kept plus–minus, and as a goalie you are ineligible for the Widgeon Award.

—The what? about five of us asked.

—It's his own award, Beckstein said, which he presents in a personal ceremony to the player who leads his daughter's team in that particular, much-underrated statistic. He buys a little trophy and everything.

—Who won last year? I asked.

—Sandy did, said Pincher. And don't let him pretend he didn't keep the trophy. It's probably the only one he'll ever get and he knows it.

—As a matter of fact, Beckstein said, and much to your shame for not noticing, Pincher, I snuck in here two nights after the season ended and arc-welded the figurine onto the Zamboni as a kind of hood ornament.

—No way! said Pincher.

—It's true that there is a trophy figurine on the Zamboni, Woodsie said. One that was not there last year.

Beckstein smiled smugly and said, Whoever wins this season will have to think of something different.

—If I call you Nathan, said Zip, will you call me Maria?

—Sure, Nathan said. Kiss my cup, Maria.

—Which one? Zip said. You have two.

—Three, she said.

—What's the third one for? Cody asked sincerely.

—That will cost you a quarter to find out, said Nathan. Plus a trip to the Supreme Court and a few calendars in the federal slammer.

In little bunches the rest of the guys drifted in—Ernie and Java and Prince and the Boot, who actually blushed when he looked at Nathan and, as far as I could tell, never looked at her again for the duration of the season. Most of last year's Squirts moved up to the Peewee A team, just as most of last year's Peewees went to Bantams. Only Pincher and Sandy and the girl are left from last year's Peewee team, which went about .500.

—Hey, goalie, said Sandy. Is your hundred-goal pal Moseby a Peewee this year, or did he stay a Squirt?

—Oh, he's a Peewee, said Zip. His birthday's two weeks before mine.

Sandy cussed bitterly and said, Well, there go the Montrose games. Then, as if on cue, Kenny Moseby himself walked into the room with his bag on his shoulder, nodding a shy hello to everyone.

Sandy gaped. Is he—Are you playing for *us*? he said.

—Why else would he be here, Foamface? Zip said.

Sandy hooted and threw both fists in the air. Kenny tried to ignore him by digging into his bag, but I saw his neck blush.

—Looks like you can kiss those hopes of repeating as the Widgeon winner good-bye, said Woodsie. Then he walked over and quietly introduced himself to Kenny with a handshake and a few murmured words. It was a formality—they played against each other several times last year—but it's just the sort of gentlemanly touch Woodsie would see was needed to break the wowie-zowie bit Beckstein started. It worked; nobody else reacted to Kenny's presence except by saying hello, or Welcome back. His neck went back to its normal color.

—Politeness, said Cody, shaking his head. Sensitivity. Jeez, it's going to be a funny year.

—Oh, goody! Zip squealed. I just *adore* humor! Does anyone know any off-color limericks?

—There once was a team from Wolf*bay*—I started.

—Stop it right *now*, said Zip, or I will honest to goodness wet my *pants*.

—You people are peculiar, said Nathan.

The Boot just shook his head and got dressed. Moseby pulled on his skates. Woodsie, all dressed, leaned silently against the wall. Barry looked around in general disgust. The door swung open and for a second no one was there. Then Shinny hopped in on crutches with one leg in a long cast.

—Oh, great! said Barry with even more disgust, throwing a sock into his bag. What happened to you?

—Bessaball been berry berry good to me, said Shinny, as he dropped to a bench and propped his busted leg on his crossed crutches.

—You broke your leg playing *baseball*? Zip asked incredulously.

—Yep.

—What happened? asked Cody. Like, a high-speed, blindside collision in the outfield or something?

—Something like that, Shinny said.

—Nonsense, said Woodsie. We all looked at him. I was at the game because my sister plays on the other team. Shinny took a huge cut at a change-up, missed it by a foot, and somehow managed to smash himself in the leg with his aluminum bat. And I mean smash it *fat*, said Woodsie. He got it *all*.

Shinny shrugged.

Kenny was staring at Shinny in utter disbelief. To Kenny there is no sport—in fact, no reason for breathing—other than ice hockey. Shinny gave him a wave and said, Hey, K. Still good for three hundred points?

Moseby blushed and dropped his eyes.

—Who's coaching? Shinny asked. I heard they canned your old man, Codes.

—Yeah, said Cody, pulling his sweater over his head. He wasn't macho enough with us last year. Didn't show that hunger to win that we all like to see on a Wolfbay team.

—Right, I said. That special hunger and brilliant strategies that just *might* have turned some of those twelve-goal losses into ten-goal losses.

—Did they really blame your *dad*? Shinny said. We reeked, all by ourselves.

—And it was only thanks to him we got better at the end, said Barry.

—No, no, said Zip. That was the goaltending.

Ignoring him, Prince said, Even my grandfather

was impressed with Coach Cooper.

There was a moment of awed silence while the profound import of this sank in for the new Peewees. We all know Prince's grandfather well, and know that almost *nothing* impresses him, though he notices absolutely everything that happens on the ice in every practice and game and is not at all shy about giving you a very precise lecture about how you should have never been holding your stick blade against the ice at a certain angle even though the puck was in the corner ninety feet away, because if the puck happened to strike your stick blade just *so* . . . Nobody minds these lectures, largely because we all really like Prince's grandfather and appreciate his attention but also because usually by the third sentence he has gotten so excited he has forgotten to speak English and the rest comes in his cool-sounding French, at approximately eight words a second.

—Your grandfather comes to the games? asked Nathan. I imagine she is thinking Prince, being a black hockey player and therefore a bizarre aberration in his family, was probably scorned by all his bloods, who must play basketball instead.

Common mistake.

—His grandfather comes to *showers*, said Cody.

—We don't have showers in our locker rooms, Cody.

—But if we did, said Prince, it is true that my grandpop would probably be unable in certain crucial cases to restrain himself from following whoever he was talking to about the misplaced center of gravity of a second-period hipcheck right under the spray.

—In his suit, of course, said Zip.

—*Not* taking time to remove the silk pocket handkerchief, said Woodsie.

I looked at Nathan and said, His grandfather was born in Montreal, so hockey is kind of important to him.

—That's a city in France, Zip added helpfully. So he mostly speaks French.

—They *love* hockey over there across the great Atlantic, said Cody.

—Yeah, said Prince. When I think of the number of great French players who have filled NHL rosters since—

The door opened and again there was a delay

before the person opening it showed himself. This time, jumping quickly through and into the room and flattening himself along the wall, looking over his shoulder at the door and panting, it was Cody's dad, wearing his warm-ups and skates but also one of those ten-cent fake nose-mustache-glasses things.

—Help! said Zip, putting a hand to his forehead. I suddenly feel I am about to fall in love with losing for losing's sake!

—De*feat* is *sweet*, Woodsie chanted, joined by four or five others.

Coach Cooper pulled off the disguise. Hello, Peewees, he said. And thanks for the welcome. You guys would mock a double amputee.

—First we'd challenge him to a footrace, Zip said.

—What if the 'double' referred to his arms, and he still had both legs? Prince asked.

—Then, after he beat me in the footrace, I would pound the crap out of him with both of *my* hands.

—Are you our coach? asked Kenny, sounding hopeful.

—I have that honor, Coach Coop said with a bow. All the old Squirts cheered. He held up his hands to stop us.

—But I must warn you, he said, that I am not the same old softy you so craftily enjoy taking advantage of. No. It is true that the fellow who was going to coach you came down with mononucleosis, and that there was absolutely no one else the board could think of who would bear the insult of being asked to step in so late, *but*—he shakes a finger at us—I have been given this opportunity only if I promise to become a nastier, shiftier, more cutthroat kind of guy. So be warned: This season, I am pulling out every trick in the bag—we are going hell-bent for that elusive nineteen-loss figure, no matter what the cost to your self-esteem.

We all cheered. You're *just* the guy who can lose only nineteen, said Shinny. We all have faith in you.

—Even these ringers from last year's team, said Zip, looking at the three of them, who mostly didn't know what to think or do. Isn't that *right*? he yelled.

—Certainly, said Sandy. I would definitely get behind a team goal of losing less than twenty-nine.

—Count me in, said Nathan. I'm *much* more of

a nineteen-loss kind of player.

Pincher was out of his league, though. Frowning, trying hard to get it, he said, Do we, like, *have* to lose nineteen?

—It's a point of honor, said Woodsie. Didn't you hear the man?

—Could we maybe lose even fewer? Pincher asked meekly.

We all started lecturing him in nonsense at once, until Coach tooted his whistle. We all shut up and looked at him.

—I want you on the ice in sixty seconds, he said, and then left.

A couple of guys cussed and hustled to tie their skates and snap their helmets, whatever the last steps were, and everyone else crowded the door. Pincher was still sitting, perplexed.

—This guy jokes with you like that, he coaches you to the worst season anybody ever had in this club—but when he says jump, you still jump?

—He's the coach, Pinch, I said.

Pinch shook his head, but then he jammed his helmet on in a hurry and made it onto the ice in time.

two

We weren't too bad for the first skate, really. We were all different in this practice than we were in tryouts; everybody knows this was our first real look at each other. Because almost the whole team was together last year, there weren't any big surprises. Still, a couple of things stood out.

One was that Nathan can really fly. In fact, she's not only extremely fast, she can maneuver really well in tight spaces, what's called "making ice for yourself," and backwards she may be almost as fast as Cody. I am impressed. But I would be even more impressed if she kept her stick blade on the ice or held her stick with both hands all the time or showed some of that sudden sprint-speed when a puck got past her into a corner. Nathan showed no inclination to get in there and fight for it when it's all elbows and butts and knees. I tried not to be sexist about this.

The second surprise, as always, was just how

incredible Kenny Moseby is. Not just how *good* he is, which is amazing enough; but how inspired and fresh and excited he is, acting as if every drill is going to be his final chance to experience the joys of ice-skating in his life. It's not "acting" as in "faking." This is how K lives, once he has skates on: nothing is done except at full speed, with reckless abandon. He hurls himself after every loose puck, he spins tight as a geometry lesson around every cone, he skates all the way to each line in line drills—while everyone else kind of cheats and stops a little short and a little soft and coasts to within a foot or two, Kenny skates to the line and stops dead on it from full tilt to zero in one big spray, but before the crystals have fallen he has taken off back to the next line. If we had anyone but Coach Coop, who has known K since he was about four, we'd probably all think Moze was kissing up and making us all look bad. But Coach knows better than to expect the rest of us humans to match Kenny. He also knows that being around Kenny *does* tend to make anyone go a *little* harder than he otherwise might, out of a feeling that arises somewhere between competitiveness and inspiration.

Everything else was usual. Zip was moaning and

sitting down and stuff, acting like he generally had a harder job than anybody and got paid way less. Plus he was panting from skating half the length of the ice at half-speed on his way to the cage.

—Zip, said the Coach at one point. Do you know what your best single feature is?

—That would be the unique color of my eyes, Zip said, which is a very rare shade of blue often called 'cobalt'—

—Your best feature, at least the only one I can figure keeps landing you on travel teams, is being the son of the rink manager, said Coach. How in the world—I mean, it was *nice* out this summer— how did you manage to avoid getting into any kind of playing condition?

—Practice, Coach, said Zip. A careful regimen of practice, practice, practice. You'd be surprised what an inert slug you can become if you work hard enough at it.

I noticed Prince had grown some over the summer and gotten stronger—the first couple of times I tried to pry him off the puck in a corner using the same leverage and effort that had worked last year, he just shrugged me off. That was good.

I noticed Cody, already the smallest player on the team, seemed to have maybe shrunk by a couple of inches. That was not good. But then, Codes is such a supreme skater that there is almost no one who can get enough of a hold on him to apply any muscle.

Woodsie and Billy had obviously been to camp. Woodsie had just as obviously spent a good few hours thinking about the game, whereas Billy had clearly *not* thought about it one second beyond zipping his bag. Billy's dad is always talking hockey to him, and I believe Billy lets that take the place of doing any thinking on his own.

In our first okay-let's-really-try scrimmage, the Blacks beat the Blues 8–2. Kenny, who did not seem to dominate the game in any particular way, scored seven of those goals. Seven. Looking back as carefully as you like, you could not say you have the memory of him carrying the puck more than anybody else, nor could you recall grand rushes in which he wound his way resolutely through the entire defense, driven by pure will to the inevitable score. You just remember he was always in the right spot, playing his position; he always had his head up and his stick down; he always played hard. And somehow it added up to the astonishing number of seven goals.

Maybe it's because I'm a defenseman, but probably not—in any case, if I look back and remember any particular play of Kenny's during a game or scrimmage, it's almost always a defensive play. He always shuts down his own man, but keeps one eye on the rest of the ice and the guys and the puck and where everything is and how fast it's moving in which direction, so when danger is about to strike because somebody gets turned around or misjudges an angle for a check, well, then suddenly Kenny is on the spot to backcheck a two-on-one into a harmless two-on-two, or to poke-check a rushing winger with one awkwardly turned man to beat at the blue line for a breakaway.

Those are my favorite K-plays, and *they* don't even show up in his stats. They show up on the scoreboard, though, as "non goals," and in close games they can be decisive.

I make a point of mentioning several of these plays to Kenny whenever I'm on the ice with him, because I suspect he likes the semi-secrecy of them better than the gaudy goals–assists totals he always rings up, which anyone can see and gawk over. He always thanks me and mumbles something about getting lucky, but we both know better.

I like to think that if I were the best player in the area, maybe one of the best fifty in the country, I would be all shy and blushy like Kenny. But I probably wouldn't. Probably, I'd strut and trumpet, never letting my lips go cold, as Zip puts it when he marvels at my active mouth.

Actually, there are times when my mouth is useful in a hockey game: I chatter at opponents and if one of them is a hothead who can be distracted by words, I will get him off his game; I talk to my teammates, and with them I don't just mess—it is important to communicate on coverage, pass options, all kinds of things; and lastly, I sometimes talk to the referee and linesmen. Not to whine, and not to ask for obvious favors and stuff like that, but to mention a foul an opponent is getting away with behind their backs, or to calmly disagree with an offside call, or to represent the team's interests when something complicated is being called.

Secretly—one would never be vocal about *this*— I hope my mouth will get me elected captain of the team this year.